A Letter for Maria

by Elizabeth Lindsay
illustrations by Alex de Wolf

Orchard Books · A division of Franklin Watts, Inc.
New York and London

Bear is sad.
The sun is shining
and the sky is blue.
But nothing's any fun
without his friend
Maria.

Bear can't write, so he paints a picture-letter for Maria. It has flowers, blue sky, a butterfly, and a friendly bear in it. Guess who?

Bear walks along the street carrying his letter.
Maybe he's taking it to the post office.

Watch out, Bear!
Oh, no! Splash!
Bear is now very wet.

Bear drips onto the sidewalk.
He's making a puddle.
Even his letter is soaking wet.
But he decides to go on.

Bear sees a butterfly flutter past. "Just like the one in my letter," he thinks. Slowly the sun dries his furry coat.

Bear arrives outside a large building. He's looking for something.

It's not the post office
after all. It's the hospital.

"Excuse me, I want to see my friend, Maria. Which way do I go?" The nurse tells Bear to follow the arrows and climb the stairs to room 120.

Bear walks along the hall. Room 1-2-0. He looks for another arrow. "Go that way," says a passing doctor.

Bear climbs the stairs.
He hopes he's headed in
the right direction.
The arrow points up.
So up he goes.

What is the number
on the door?
Bear looks carefully.
This is it.

Inside the room are
two high beds. Bear can't
see who is in them.

"Bear," cries a voice.
"Is that you?"
  Bear holds up the letter.

"Thank you, Bear," says Maria,
  holding him tight.
"I've missed you, Maria,"
  whispers Bear.
"I've missed you too," says Maria.
  Bear gives Maria a bear hug
  that lasts a very long time.

Orchard Books, 387 Park Avenue South, New York, New York 10016

Orchard Books is a division of Franklin Watts, Inc.

Manufactured in the United States of America
Book design by Susan Detrich. The text of this book is set in 24 pt ITC New Baskerville
The illustrations are pencil and watercolor, reproduced in halftone
10 9 8 7 6 5 4 3 2 1

Library of Congress Cataloging-in-Publication Data

Lindsay, Elizabeth. A letter for Maria. Summary: Maria's teddy bear seeks her out to bring
her a picture letter when she is in the hospital. [1. Teddy bears—Fiction. 2. Hospitals—Fiction]
I. Title   PZ7.L6598Le 1988   [E]   88-1641 ISBN 0-531-05775-5   ISBN 0-531-08375-6 (lib. bdg.)